Callie Polly-Oli Cow

Alycia R. Wright

To order additional copies of this book, contact:
Bookwhip
1-855-339-3589
https://www.bookwhip.com

Callie Polly-Oli Cow
was a dame so curt and cute.
She courted counts of charming chaps,
in their best of Sunday suits.

RING!
RING!
RING!

There were chaps calling in her courtyard.
Some carried candies, cards, and boxes.
They came to charm ol' Callie
with their cell phones, cars, and faxes.

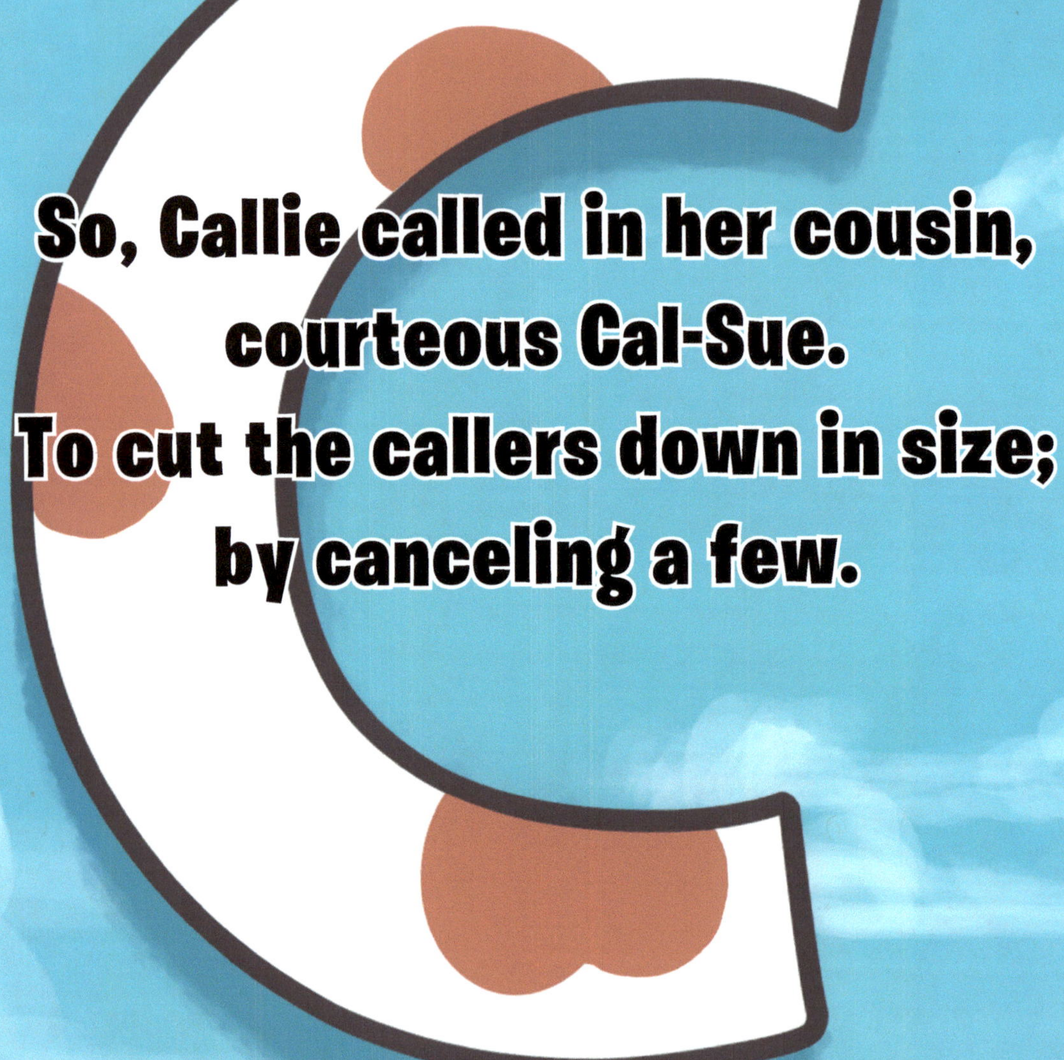

So, Callie called in her cousin,
courteous Cal-Sue.
To cut the callers down in size;
by canceling a few.

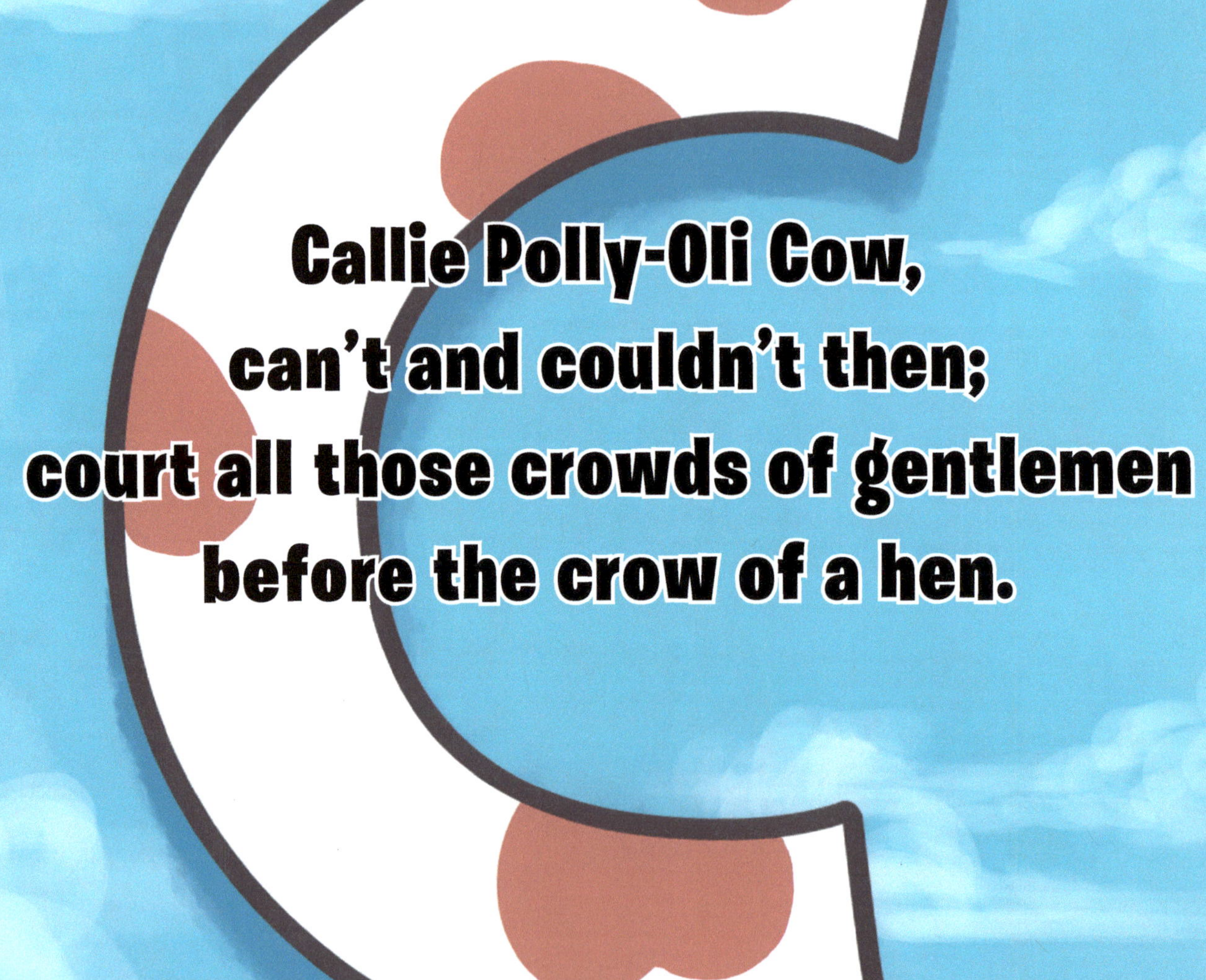

Callie Polly-Oli Cow,
can't and couldn't then;
court all those crowds of gentlemen
before the crow of a hen.

One day a chap came calling.
Named Captain Carly Clam.
The Captain had read about dear Callie Cow.
Carly had come to take her hand.

Carly crossed the crafty ocean,
leaving Cala-lama-loo.
To beg Callie's hand in marriage.
He adored and loved her too.

USA

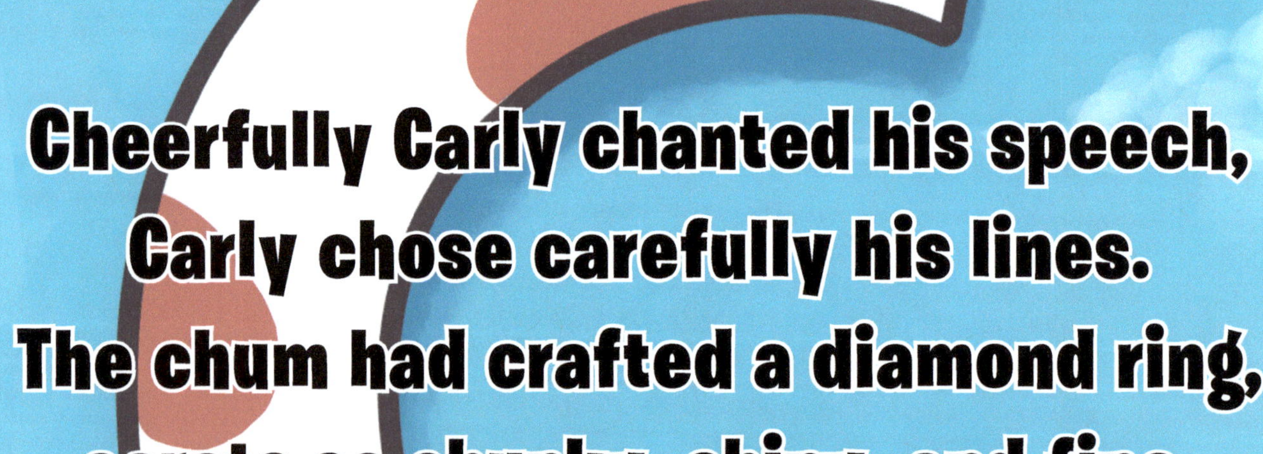

Cheerfully Carly chanted his speech,
Carly chose carefully his lines.
The chum had crafted a diamond ring,
carats so chunky, shiny, and fine.

INA
HAWAII
FR
AFRICA
IT

When Carly's turn came for calling,
he tipped his cap and cheesed.
"Dearest Callie Polly-Oli Cow,
Marry me. Will you please?"

You know: dear Ol'classy Callie
did not have a clue.
She could think of no good reason;
to make Captain Carly blue.

So, she chose to accept his charming chide.
She packed all her things and then;
Callie placed a sign upon her door.
CLOSED: I've found a chum.

"No longer am I courting.
I have accepted and said, "I do."
I have married a clammy suitor,
from Cala-lama-loo."

19

www.ingramcontent.com/pod-product-compliance
Lightning Source LLC
Chambersburg PA
CBHW041926180726
48295CB00003B/86